MW00763472

This book belongs to:

_____

A keepworthy gift from:

_____

Published by Keepworthy Creations LLC
6733 N. Post Oak Road, Peoria, IL 61615
www.keepworthy.com

Distributed by Keepworthy Creations LLC.

Critters Like Me™ is a trademark of Keepworthy Creations LLC

Library of Congress Control Number: 2011916168

ISBN-13: 978-0-9833155-2-0

For more information about Keepworthy Creations' fine gifts and books, visit
www.keepworthy.com.

RANDALL'S CHRISTMAS VISION

Written by
Betty Counce

Illustrated by
Dave Seay

In all the famous Christmas stories, the only reindeer you hear about are the ones who guide Santa's sleigh. But there are important reindeer who work *behind* the scenes, too. And one of those reindeer is me. My name is Randall. I'm pretty easy to spot—I'm the only reindeer at the North Pole who wears big, thick black-rimmed glasses.

You see, ever since I was born I've had poor vision, which made it hard

for me to keep up with my friends. Many times I felt like giving up. Then my dad taught me about confidence. He said having confidence means that if you believe in yourself, you can do almost anything. I tried my best to follow his advice.

In time, however, forest life became too dangerous for me. Lots of hungry wolves were roaming around, just waiting for a reindeer who couldn't see them coming. So, my mom went into the village to ask a favor of her good friends Santa and Mrs. Claus. They agreed to take me into their home and look after me like I was their own. It was there that my confidence really grew.

The first thing Santa did was have the elves fit me with glasses. They were the ones who picked out my big black frames. At first I didn't know if I liked the glasses, but Mrs. Claus assured me how smart and stylish they made me look.

In order to earn some money, I began cooking and cleaning up around the house. I loved the Clauses dearly, but I soon grew bored with being their butler. I longed to do something more with my life. I wanted to prove that I could be a part of something truly great, even with my poor eyesight.

That's why I was so excited when Santa announced a new job opening one Christmas. You see, a long time ago Christmas was quite different than it is today. For one thing, Santa didn't own a sleigh. And when he delivered toys to children's homes, he didn't put the gifts under a tree. Nobody even knew what a Christmas tree was.

When Santa made his announcement, he and Mrs. Claus were sitting at the kitchen table while I was fixing their morning cups of hot chocolate. "As you both know," Santa said, "I usually deliver the Christmas toys on my own. But the children's wish lists are getting longer and longer, so this year I bought a

sleigh. And now I need to pick some animals to guide it. Do you have any ideas?"

"How about penguins?" asked Mrs. Claus. "They are such cute little things."

"Penguins?!" Santa roared. "I can't use penguins to guide my sleigh! Penguins live at the *South* Pole."

"Oh, my," she said. "I think you're right. That would explain why I haven't seen any around here."

"What about reindeer?" I asked, pushing their cups onto the table with my nose. "They are very smart and strong. And I can tell you which ones would be the best workers since I used to live with them in the forest."

"That sounds great," said Santa. "But could you have nine of them here by tonight? I need a full day to train them before Christmas Eve."

"No problem," I said. "I can leave for the forest right away."

"Wonderful," he said. "I'll assign one of the elves to go with you."

I cheered with delight. "Oh, thank you, Santa, thank you! The reindeer will be so thrilled!"

I left the Clauses' and trotted toward my old home. My plan was to bring back only *eight* reindeer. That way, Santa would have to choose *me* as the ninth. There wouldn't be enough time to go back and get another.

The eight reindeer I chose were excited about the job and gladly followed me back to the Clauses. When we arrived, I left them outside

while I went in to talk with the boss. I found him and Mrs. Claus sitting up in bed drinking their evening cups of hot chocolate.

"Your new guiding team is waiting out front for you, sir," I said.

"All nine of them?" he asked.

I took a deep breath. "Well, sir, I only have eight. But that's okay, because I volunteer to be the ninth guider myself." I pushed my glasses up on my nose and stuck my chest out proudly.

"Oh, no, Randall dear," said Mrs. Claus. "We can't let you do that. It would be too dangerous with your poor eyesight."

"But I can do it!" I said with confidence. "I'm just as strong as the other reindeer, and the moonlight will help me see. Please, Santa?"

"I'm sorry, Randall," he said, "but I'm afraid Mrs. Claus is right. Delivering toys on Christmas Eve is a very long and difficult journey."

"I know it is. But I'm ready for it! I'll work ten times as hard as the others. And I'll be safe—I promise!" I crossed my hooves and pleaded.

"Look, Randall," he said, "we promised your parents we would keep you safe. Besides, my guiders must be ready for anything, and I can't take the chance that your poor eyesight might put us in danger. I will just

have to get by with only eight reindeer."

My heart sank. "Well, I'll go tell the others you're ready for them," I said.

"Oh, Santa," sighed Mrs. Claus. "I can't bear to see our little Randall so unhappy. Isn't there *something* he can do for you on Christmas?"

"Well…" Santa said, stroking his long beard. "Not that I can think of."

"It's okay," I said, hanging my head. "I understand. There's nothing important for a reindeer like me to do on Christmas Eve. I'll just get started on the winter cleaning. If you'll excuse me, I think the big vacuum is in the village hall."

"That's it!" cried Mrs. Claus, clasping her hands together. "Randall can be in charge of decorating the village hall!" She was so tickled.

Santa didn't look as pleased. Decorating the hall was supposed to be *her* job. She did it every year.

"Santa, dear," she continued, "you know how much I've always wanted to go shopping during the Christmas Eve sales. I'm usually too busy to leave the village, but if Randall fills in for me…"

I couldn't believe my ears. Next to guiding Santa's sleigh, this was probably the most important job at the North Pole! The village hall is where the big party takes place on Christmas morning. Everyone would be there to see my decorations. My confidence was returning. "Oh, please, Santa!" I begged. "Can I do it?"

Santa stroked his beard again, thinking. I knew he felt bad for turning me down to guide his sleigh. "All right," he finally said.

"Yippee!" I shouted, jumping with joy. "Thanks, Santa. You won't regret it!"

"I better not," he said. "It's a very important job. You will be responsible for setting the mood of the entire holiday."

"Yes, sir, I understand. The hall will look the best it ever has—you'll see!" I turned and galloped to my room. Even though I was excited, I tried to get some sleep. I knew I had a busy day ahead of me.

I left the house first thing in the morning. If I wanted the hall to look its best, I couldn't decorate it on my own, so I called on my four best friends: Ollie the owl, Posey the polar bear, and twin squirrel brothers named Scoot and Scamper. They were all eager to help.

We met at a picnic table in the village square, the grounds just outside the hall. Scoot and Scamper sat on one bench, Posey sat on the other, and Ollie perched in a nearby tree. I stood at the head of the table. "All right," I said, "the first order of business is to choose a theme—an idea that ties all of our decorations together."

"We have an idea!" squeaked Scoot.

"Yeah, we have a great idea," echoed his brother Scamper. "This year's theme should be 'Squirrels'. All the decorations can be brown and fluffy just like us." They looked at each other with wide grins on their little faces.

"A squirrel theme?" scoffed Ollie. "That's the silliest idea I've heard!"

"It's not bad," I said, "but it wouldn't be fair to the rest of the critters in the forest."

"What about the forest itself?" asked Posey. "I think the pine trees are the

prettiest things in the village."

"I like the bushes with the red berries," said Ollie.

"What about the snowflakes?" questioned Scoot.

"And the icicles!" cried Scamper.

I was very proud of my team. "I think we could use all those ideas to make some great decorations," I said.

"But I don't understand," Scoot said, frowning.

"Yeah, I don't understand either," said Scamper. "If we decorate the hall like a forest, won't the *inside* of the hall just look like the *outside*?"

"You nitwits," said Ollie. "That's the whole point! The forest has great natural beauty. But it's so cold here that most people don't stay outside long enough to enjoy it."

"So we should try to bring some of that beauty inside," added Posey.

"Exactly," I said. "I think it's a great idea. What do you say, guys?" I looked at the squirrel brothers.

"It's not as good as the squirrel idea," said Scoot, "but it'll do."

"Yeah, it'll do," said Scamper.

"Wonderful," I said. "We'll begin making the decorations after lunch. But first, I need you to spread a message to the villagers. I want everyone to bring their own personal ornament to the Christmas party. That way, the whole village will have a part in the decorating."

While my team went to spread the word, I stayed behind in the square. I tried to think how I could make the Christmas party a truly magical event. Suddenly, my eyes twinkled and my antlers twitched as the perfect vision came to mind. I hurried off to start the preparations.

When I got back to the square, there was a big box of decorating supplies waiting for me. Mrs. Claus had dropped them off before she left the village. Once the others returned, we got to work right away.

Ollie flew around from bush to bush, collecting the biggest, roundest, and brightest red berries she could find. She carefully poked a hole into each one and threaded them all together on a long piece of string.

Scoot tore open a stack of white paper. He folded each sheet in half twice and cut out lots of fun shapes along the edges. When he opened them up, they looked just like big snowflakes, each one with a unique design.

Scamper jumped onto a spool of foil and unrolled it with his feet. He

ripped the shiny paper into dozens of thin strips that looked just like the icicles hanging from the rooftops.

Posey and I walked through the square, picking up evergreen branches and pine cones. We wove the branches into thick rings and placed the cones here and there among the needles. Then we topped each ring with a bow of bright red ribbon.

When all the decorations were finished, we gathered them together and climbed the front steps to the hall. Everyone was anxious to get inside and start the decorating. Posey pushed down on the handle to the front door. "It's locked!" she cried, turning around with wide eyes.

"Oh, no!" moaned the squirrel brothers.

"It can't be locked," said Ollie, flying her way past the others. She pushed on the handle with her wing, and sure enough, it wouldn't budge. "Oh, that silly Mrs. Claus!" Ollie growled. "She must have forgotten to open it before she left."

"Then we have a big problem," I said. "Mr. and Mrs. Claus are the only ones with keys. By the time they get back, it'll be too late to decorate."

My team was very disappointed. They had all worked so hard.

"I was really looking forward to seeing how it turned out," said Posey. "I think we could have made the hall look almost as beautiful as the forest itself."

"That's it!" I shouted. "Why don't we just decorate out here?"

"Out here?" asked Posey "But where will we hang the decorations?"

"What about there?" I raised my hoof toward the tall evergreen in the middle of the square.

"On the *tree*?" asked Scoot. "That's crazy."

"Yeah, crazy," said Scamper. "No one decorates *trees*."

"Oh, hush, you two," said Ollie. "I don't think it's a bad idea. Besides, it would be better to hang our decorations out here than nowhere at all."

"Exactly," I said. "Now let's go make that tree look as great as we can!"

Ollie picked up the string of berries with her beak. She flew to the bottom of the tree and started draping the berries around the branches. At each turn she flew a little higher until she reached the very top.

The squirrels were next. Scoot hung the snowflakes around his wrists, and Scamper stuffed as many icicles as he could into his fists.

They jumped onto the lowest branch of the tree and began hanging their decorations carefully among the needles. They climbed in steady circles all the way to the top.

Meanwhile, Posey and I got busy putting up our evergreen rings. We hung the largest one on the front door of the hall. The stunning dark green pine really made the building come to life.

At last, it was time to place our personal ornaments on the tree.

To honor their original theme idea, Scoot and Scamper hung up two squirrels made from brown cotton balls. Ollie hung up a frame of owl feathers with a picture of her family in the middle. Posey hung up a straw sled to show how much she enjoyed playing in the snow. "Where's yours?" Ollie asked me.

"Santa's getting mine," I answered. "He'll have it at the party when he returns from delivering the toys."

"But what is it?" Scoot asked.

"Yeah, what's the ornament?" asked Scamper.

"You'll have to wait and see," I said.

"Oh, goody, I love surprises," said Posey.

"Speaking of surprises," I said, pointing to my watch, "it's almost midnight! We should head home and get some sleep. The party starts very early tomorrow."

When the elves rang the bell the next morning, my team and I were the first ones at the square. As the villagers arrived, Ollie flew over them and announced: "The hall can't be opened until Santa gets back, so we're hanging the ornaments on a tree. Please place your gifts under the branches so they won't get wet from the falling snow. And Merry Christmas!"

Everyone told us how wonderful the tree looked as they lined up with
excitement to hang their ornaments. Each one was special and unique.
There was everything from angels to drums to candy canes. No one had

heard of decorating a tree before, but they all thought it was a fun and festive idea.

Suddenly we heard bells jingling in the distance, and everyone looked toward the sky. "Ho, ho, ho!" Santa yelled as his sleigh came into view. "Merry Christmas!"

Everyone cheered. It was time to start the party!

Santa and his reindeer landed at the edge of the

square. He opened the door, plopped down onto the snow, and walked straight over to me and my team. "This looks marvelous!" he said, waving his hand at the big tree. "The decorations are absolutely beautiful. What a clever idea to hang them on a tree!"

We thanked him for his kindness. Then Posey explained why we hadn't decorated inside the hall.

"No worries," Santa said. "Once I unlock it, we'll just take the decorations inside."

"Take them inside?" asked Scoot.

"But the decorations are on a tree," said Scamper. "We can't just take them inside!"

"Ho, ho, ho," Santa chuckled. "Sure we can. We'll just have the elves cut down the tree. Then we can plant a new one to replace it."

"But all the decorations will fall off!" hooted Ollie.

Santa grinned. "You just leave that to me."

Out of the crowd jumped two elves, a saw already in their hands. After clearing the way, they cut down the tree in three big swipes. The rest of the elves rushed in, lifted the tree, and carried it up the front steps of the hall. One elf stayed behind to drop a single seed into the hole where the tree used to be. He sprinkled it with a tiny water can and kicked some soil over the top.

As Santa promised, all the decorations stayed in place on the tree. Not a single piece moved. When Ollie demanded to know how this had happened, Santa answered, "It's simply the magic of Christmas."

Everyone stared in awe as they entered the hall. The tree stood grandly in the center of the room with the presents peeking out from beneath. The branches reached to the ceiling, and the sweet smell of pine filled the air. The decorations looked even prettier than they had outside.

I was admiring all the ornaments when Mrs. Claus tapped me on the shoulder. She had just returned from her trip. "Randall, dear," she said, looking confused, "Ollie just told me how you couldn't get into the hall last night. But I am almost positive I unlocked the door before I left."

"I thought you did, too, Mrs. Claus. But sometimes things just happen." I tried to hide my smile.

"Oh, well. It doesn't really matter," she said. "Santa couldn't be more

pleased with the decorations. And I've never seen the villagers so full of Christmas spirit."

"I'm so glad," I said. "I was sad when Santa turned me down as a guider, but once I started planning the decorations, I knew it was the job I was really meant to have."

"You know what else is odd?" asked Mrs. Claus. "I've lost my key to the village hall. I always keep it in the same place at home, but now I can't find it anywhere." She paused for a moment. "Randall, you don't think someone took the key and locked the hall on purpose, do you? Wouldn't that be the silliest thing!"

"Maybe not *so* silly," I mumbled to myself.

As everyone lined up for snacks, I quietly slipped out the back door, trotted over to the Clauses' house, and climbed the stairs to their room. From a hiding spot in my antlers, I pulled out a small key. I hung it in the cabinet next to the bed and smiled. Mrs. Claus would be crazy with wonder at how the key had safely returned, just like it had never left.

I reentered the hall as

Santa was telling everyone to get quiet. "I have a big surprise for you all," he said with a sparkle in his eyes. "We have one more ornament to hang." The elves carried his giant toy sack into the room. Santa reached into the bag and pulled out something that gave off a magnificent golden glow.

Everyone gasped. What on earth could it be?

"A STAR!" cried Posey. "A *real* star from the sky!"

"That's the surprise you were talking about, isn't it, Randall?" asked Ollie.

I nodded, too excited to respond.

"It's wonderful!" said Scoot.

"Just wonderful!" echoed Scamper.

The villagers were stunned when Santa tossed the star into the air and it landed gently on the very top of the tree. The sparkling light shined down on each and every ornament.

Everyone stared in amazement. They had never seen anything so beautiful. The star was truly a blessing. Its warm glow symbolized the love that each family held in their hearts.

As the party continued, I studied the crowd through my handsome black glasses. Everyone was smiling and enjoying themselves, discussing what kind of ornament they would bring next year. It was then I knew that my Christmas vision would become a cherished tradition.

My Scrapbook Pages

Draw and color

your favorite ornament or your family's Christmas tree!

Letter to Santa

BAXTER'S BIG TEETH

The official tooth box companion gift for the first book in the Critters Like Me collection

Baxter's Tooth Fairy Tooth Box

Just in case you forgot to purchase the companion gift to Baxter's Big Teeth, it's on sale now! Children can use this box, embossed with Baxter's acorn, to store their baby teeth for the Tooth Fairy. It makes the perfect companion gift to the book or an eclectic addition to your autumn décor.

To purchase this heirloom-quality gift, go to www.keepworthy.com. View the latest prices at the secure online store and browse for upcoming titles in the Critters Like Me collection.

Personally designed by Christopher Hovey
Tooth box contains pewter finish and a black velvet liner.
Gift includes a suede-finish bag for long-term storage.
2.5 in. Dia. X 1.125 in. H

Critters Like Me™

Critters Like Me™

Keepworthy Creations will continue to add books to the Critters Like Me Collection. Don't miss this upcoming title in 2012!

Spring 2012 Penny Takes Flight

For years Penny the Penguin has enjoyed watching the birds fly over her snowy island home. Being a bird herself, she doesn't understand why she can't fly with the others. Her parents' explanations only make her feel worse. She is determined to fly and makes many failed attempts to do so, including tying herself to a kite.

One day, a pilot is forced to land his plane on the island. Afterwards, Penny's life is never the same again.

Visit the website at **www.keepworthy.com** to view the the latest updates on our book-related giftlines and other keepsake products and services.

Betty Counce - Author

Betty Counce is a southern belle with a heart of gold and a love for teaching children. She has over 30 years of teaching experience in speech, drama, reading, and writing. Not a day goes by without her getting hugs from current or former students and hearing, "Mrs. Counce, you were my favorite teacher," and "You were so cool!"

Her knowledge and experience leaves no doubt that authoring children's books is the best place for her to be. Her authoring and promotion of reading literacy leaves little time for thoughts of retirement. Betty lives with her husband, Bob, in central Illinois and is a partner in Keepworthy Creations LLC.

Dave Seay - Illustrator

Keepworthy Creations is proud to have Dave Seay as the illustrator for the entire Critters Like Me™ collection of books. Dave has over 40 years of experience in fine art and illustration.

His work has been featured in magazines, newspapers, books and many other forms of media across the country. He also paints fine art landscapes and many of them are featured in corporate collections. This is his first experience in illustrating a children's book. Dave lives in Peoria, Illinois, with his wife and two cats. He has three grown children and a grandson.

Chris Hovey - Designer

Chris Hovey is a graduate of Robert Morris University and is an accomplished graphic designer, photographer and 3-D generalist. His degrees in business admininstration and graphic design have prepared him well to flourish in the publishing business.

He has over 11 years of professional experience in graphic design with specialization in 3-D modeling. He will design and sculpt Keepworthy Creation's Gift collections using 3-D software. He has a diverse portfolio of commercial stock photography and photorealistic 3-D renders for major consumer packaged goods companies. Chris is a partner with Keepworthy Creations LLC. He currently lives and works in central Illinois.